JALEN'S BIG CITY LIFE

SHARING THE MOUND

by **Dorothy H. Price** illustrated by **Shiane Salabie**

PICTURE WINDOW BOOKS

a capstone imprint

Published by Picture Window Books, an imprint of Capstone.
1710 Roe Crest Drive, North Mankato, Minnesota 56003
capstonepub.com

Library of Congress Cataloging-in-Publication Data is available
on the Library of Congress website
ISBN: 9781666335002 (hardcover)
ISBN: 9781666335040 (paperback)
ISBN: 9781666342031 (ebook PDF)

Summary: Baseball is J.C.'s favorite sport, so he's excited to see it on the
activity list at the local community center. He can't wait to show off what
a great pitcher he is. But then Vicky gets to be the pitcher instead. Can J.C.
learn to share the mound?

Editorial Credits
Editor: Alison Deering; Designer: Tracy Davies;
Production Specialist: Katy LaVigne

Design Elements
Shutterstock: Alexzel, Betelejze, cuppuccino, wormig

TABLE OF CONTENTS

MEET J.C.

Hi! My name is Jalen Corey Pierce, but everyone calls me J.C. I am seven years old. I live with Mom, Dad, and my baby sister, Maya. Nana and Pop-Pop live in our apartment building too. So do my two best friends, Amir and Vicky.

My family and I used to live in a small town. Now I live in a city with big buildings and lots of people. Come along with me on all my new adventures!

Chapter 1

PLAY BALL

J.C. loved going to the community center near his family's apartment building. This week, he saw a special flyer. The center was going to have a baseball team!

Baseball was J.C.'s favorite
sport. He used to play in his
old town. He already had a bat,
a glove, a helmet, and cleats.
That was everything he needed.

J.C. told Amir and Vicky.

They wanted to play too.

On Saturday, everyone met at the city field. The coach split the group into teams. Vicky, Amir, and J.C. were on the same team.

"The game will have six
innings," Coach Zach explained.
"Team one will bat first. After
three outs, we'll switch. Ready
to play ball?"

"Yes!" everyone replied.

J.C.'s team took the field first.

J.C. really wanted to pitch.

"I was the best pitcher on my old team," he told the coach.

"Vicky is going to pitch first," Coach Zach said. "But everyone will switch positions. You're at second base to start."

J.C. frowned. He was ready to show off his skills. But he did what Coach said and went to his base.

Chapter 2

STRIKE THREE

Vicky threw the first pitch.

The batter struck out.

The next batter hit a fly ball.

Amir caught it at third base.

The third batter hit the ball

to second base. J.C. caught it.

That was three outs! J.C.'s team was up to bat.

"You can bat first," Amir offered.

"Thanks! I was the best batter on my old team," J.C. said.

J.C. stepped up to the plate.

All eyes were on him.

The pitcher threw the ball. J.C. swung, but he missed. Strike one.

J.C. took a deep breath. The

pitcher threw the next ball. J.C.

missed that pitch too. Strike two.

J.C. had one more chance.

He swung for the third pitch,

but he missed—again.

"Strike three," Coach Zach

said. "J.C., you're out."

Chapter 3

HAVING FUN

J.C. felt down. He didn't get
to pitch. And he had struck out.
Baseball was not very fun.

"It's okay, J.C.," Vicky said.

"You'll get a hit next time,"
Amir added.

"I hope so," J.C. said.

Amir and Vicky batted next.
They both hit the ball. Amir got
out at third base. Vicky scored
a run.

The next batter struck out.
That was three outs. That meant
J.C.'s team was back on the field.

"J.C., your turn to pitch," said Coach Zach. "Let's see what you can do."

J.C. went to the mound.

"Come on, J.C.!" his teammates cheered. "You can do it!"

J.C. took a deep breath.

Everyone else was having fun.

He decided to have fun too.

J.C. threw the first pitch.

The ball flew over the plate.

"Strike one!" Coach called.

J.C. threw the second pitch.

The batter swung and missed.

"Strike two!" Coach called.

J.C. threw the third pitch.

"Strike three!" Coach Zach exclaimed. "You've got a great arm, J.C.!"

J.C. grinned. "Thanks, Coach! That was fun!"

Chapter 4

HOME RUN

A few innings passed. The game was tied. It was J.C.'s turn to hit.

The pitcher threw the first pitch. J.C. didn't swing his bat.

"Strike one," Coach called.

The pitcher threw the second pitch. J.C. swung his bat and missed.

"Strike two," Coach called.

"You can do it, J.C.!" Vicky hollered.

"Hit it out of the park!" said Amir.

Hearing his friends helped. The pitcher threw the third pitch. J.C. swung.

Pop! J.C.'s hit went way out to left field.

"Home run!" Coach Zach yelled.

J.C. ran around the bases.

He grinned as he crossed home

plate. His hit won the game.

"I knew you could do it, J.C." Vicky said.

"That was a great game!" Amir added. "Your home run was the best part."

"Playing *together* was the best part," J.C. said. "Thanks for making baseball fun."

GLOSSARY

batter (BAT-er)—the player whose turn it is to bat

cleat (KLEET)—a shoe with small tips on the bottom to help baseball players stop or turn quickly

flyer (FLY-uhr)—a printed piece of paper that tells about an upcoming event

home plate (HOME PLAYT)—the base that a runner must touch to score

home run (HOME RUHN)—a hit that allows the batter to go around all the bases and score a run

inning (IN-ing)—the period of time in a baseball game in which each team gets a turn to bat until they get three outs

mound (MOUND)—where the pitcher stands to throw the ball

pitcher (PICH-ur)—the player who throws the ball to the batter

strike (STRIKE)—a pitched ball that is swung at and missed, a pitched ball that is in the strike zone but not swung at, or a pitched ball that is hit foul; three strikes make an out

Select one of your favorite games. Write down the steps and add a new twist. The next time you're with friends, share your new game. Ask your friends to add a new twist too. See how many versions of your favorite game you and your friends can create.

LET'S TALK

1. Have you ever played a team sport? What sport was it? What position did you play? What did you like most about playing? What didn't you like?

2. J.C. wasn't happy when Coach Zach let Vicky pitch first. Have you ever had to wait your turn or play a position you didn't like? What did you do?

3. Do you have a favorite sports memory? Why was that moment special? Are any of your friends part of your memory?

LET'S WRITE

1. J.C., Amir, and Vicky were on the same team. Would you have wanted to be on the same team as your friends? Write a short paragraph explaining why or why not.

2. Baseball is J.C.'s favorite sport. Make a list of your favorite sports. Do the sports have anything in common?

3. J.C. felt bad when he struck out, but Amir and Vicky still rooted for him. Think of a time when you felt down and your friends cheered you on. Draw a cartoon panel of that memory.

Dorothy H. Price loves writing stories for young readers, starting with her first picture book, *Nana's Favorite Things*. A 2019 winner of the We Need Diverse Books Mentorship Program, Dorothy is also an active member of the SCBWI Carolinas. She hopes all young readers know they can grow up to write stories too.

Shiane Salabie is a Jamaica-born illustrator based in the Philadelphia tri-state area. When she moved to the United States, she discovered her first true love: the library. Shiane later realized that she wanted to bring stories to life and uses her art to do so.